THE 300

A TIME TRAVEL ADVENTURE

RILEY'S TIME TRAVEL ADVENTURES
BOOK 7

VICTORIA RUSH

VOLUME 7

RILEY'S TIME TRAVEL ADVENTURES - BOOK 7

COPYRIGHT

ALSO BY VICTORIA RUSH

Adult Fairytales:

The Enchanted Forest: An Erotic Fairytale

The Land of Giants: An Erotic Fairytale

The Dragon's Lair: An Erotic Fairytale

Witch's Brew: An Erotic Fairytale

The Mage's Spell: An Erotic Fairytale

The Mermaid Lagoon: An Erotic Fairytale

The Coven: An Erotic Fairytale

Rapunzel: An Erotic Fairytale

The Seven Dwarfs: An Erotic Fairytale

The Land of Mutants: An Erotic Fairytale

The Erotic Temple: A Sexy Fairytale (Coming Soon)

Erotica Themed Bundles:

Voyeur: Lesbian Erotica Bundle

Public Affairs: A Lesbian Anthology

Futa Fantasies: The Ladyboy Collection

Threesomes: The Lesbian Collection

Threesomes - Volume 2: The Lesbian Collection

First Time: A Lesbian Anthology

Hedonism: An Erotic Anthology

Switch Hitters: Bisexual Erotica

Taboo Erotica: The Lesbian Series

BDSM: The Lesbian Collection

Party Games: The Erotic Collection

Party Games 2: The Erotic Collection

All Girl 1: Lesbian Erotica Bundle

All Girl 2: Lesbian Erotica Bundle

All Girl 3: Lesbian Erotica Bundle

All Girl 4: Lesbian Erotica Bundle

Erotic Fairytale Bundles:

Clover's Fantasy Adventures: Books 1 - 5

Clover's Fantasy Adventures: Books 6 - 10

Erotic Fantasy:

Pirate's Bounty: A Time Travel Adventure

Wild West: A Time Travel Adventure

Private Riley: A Time Travel Adventure

Cleopatra's Secret: A Time Travel Adventure

Bounty Hunter 2125: A Time Travel Adventure

Ninja Assassin: A Time Travel Adventure

The 300: A Time Travel Adventure

Arabian Nights: An Erotic Fairytale (coming soon...)

Steamy Time Travel Bundles:

Riley's Time Travel Adventures: Books 1 - 5

Lesbian Erotica:

The Dinner Party: Lesbian Voyeur Erotica

The Darkroom: Bisexual Voyeur Erotica

Naked Yoga: Lesbian Transgender Erotica

Nude Cruise: Bisexual Voyeur Erotica

Rush Hour: Taboo Public Sex

The Girl Next Door: First Time Lesbian Erotic Romance

Girls' Camp: Lesbian Group Sex

Wet Dream: Ladyboy Fantasy Erotica

The Convent: Taboo Sex with a Nun

Sex Robot: A Dream Sex Machine

The Personal Trainer: Getting Pumped at the Gym

The Dominatrix: BDSM Lesbian Domination

Webcam Chat: Lesbian Online Sex

Paint Me: A Kinky Bodypainting Workshop

The Toy Party: Girls Sharing Sex Toys

The Costume Party: Strapping One On

Swedish Sauna: Lesbian Group Sex

The Therapist: Taboo Lesbian Erotica

Elevator Shaft: Bisexual Threesomes Erotica

Ladyboy: Lesbian Transgender Erotica

Peep Show: Lesbian Voyeur Erotica

The Dare: Public Sex Erotica

Maid Service: Lesbian Threesomes Erotica

The Hitchhiker: First Time Lesbian Erotica

The Housesitter: Spycam Lesbian Erotica

The Spa: Lesbian Group Orgy

Parlor Games: Blindfold Sex Party

The Exchange Student: First Time Lesbian Erotica

The Hostel: Bisexual Group Erotica

The Harem: Lesbian Erotic Romance

The Orient Express: Lesbian Voyeur Erotica

The First Lady: A Forbidden Lesbian Erotic Romance

The Slave: Lesbian BDSM Erotica

The Masseuse: Lesbian Sensuous Erotica

Too Close for Comfort: Lesbian Forbidden Erotica

Naked Twister: A Wild Party Game

Lexi: The Sex App (Lesbian Fantasy Erotica)

Call Girl: Lesbian Bisexual Threesomes Erotica

Circle Jill: Lesbian Masturbation Workshop

The Viewing Room: Masturbation Voyeur Erotica

Spin the Bottle: A Kinky Party Game

The Hair Salon: Lesbian Voyeur Erotica

Tribadism 1: Girls Only Sex Workshop

Tribadism 2: The Art of Scissoring

Tribadism 3: Threeway Hookups

The Kiss: A Game of Oral Sex

Pledge Week: Sorority Sisters

Carny Games 1: A Wild Sex Party

Carny Games 2: A Kinky Sex Party

Carny Games 3: An Erotic Sex Party

Dreamscape: An Artificial Reality Game

Glory Hole: Guess Who's On the Other Side

Joy Ride: A Late Night Erotic Bus Trip

The Blind Girl: An Erotic Romance(Coming Soon)

Lesbian Erotica Bundles:

Jade's Erotic Adventures: Books 1 - 5

Jade's Erotic Adventures: Books 6 - 10

Jade's Erotic Adventures: Books 11 - 15

Jade's Erotic Adventures: Books 16 - 20

Jade's Erotic Adventures: Books 21 - 25

Jade's Erotic Adventures: Books 26 - 30

Jade's Erotic Adventures: Books 31 - 35

Jade's Erotic Adventures: Books 36 - 40

Jade's Erotic Adventures: Books 41 - 45

Jade's Erotic Adventures: Books 46 - 50

Fifty Shades of Jade: Superbundle

Standalone Stories:

The Polynesian Girl: A Lesbian EroticRomance

For the uninhibited...

WANT TO AMP UP YOUR SEX LIFE?

Sign up for my newsletter to receive more free books and other steamy stuff. Discover a hundred different ways to wet your whistle!

Victoria Rush Erotica

1

———

fter her adventure in the shogun period of Japan, Riley felt herself tumbling through the time machine portal once again, wondering where she'd land this time. After a few minutes, she plopped down on a dusty courtyard surrounded by stone houses with clay-tiled roofs. While she struggled to raise herself up on her arms, she was quickly surrounded by a trio of armed soldiers wearing metal helmets and brass chestplates. Glancing around her surroundings, she noticed tall mountains rising up on every side.

"Who are you?" one of the guards said in ancient Greek, squinting at her strange-looking kimono.

"Um, my name's Riley," Riley stammered, surprised by how her time machine had once again enabled her to speak the local language.

"How did you get here?" the guard said, pointing his spear threateningly in her direction. "And what is that strange costume you're wearing?"

"It's kind of a long story," Riley said, peering around the courtyard at a group of well-muscled and scantily clad soldiers sparring with heavy swords and thick shields. "Is there someone in charge that I can talk to?"

The soldier motioned toward one of the warriors who seemed to be supervising the training of the other soldiers, and the man walked over to Riley's position, peering at the young blonde girl with a curious expression. His costume was more ornate than the other soldiers, with a feathered headdress adorning his bronze helmet, an elaborately carved breastplate, and leather ribbons hanging from the hems of his linen tunic and padded skirt. Most of his face was obscured by the curved cheek plates of his helmet, but Riley could see his piercing blue eyes and square-set jaw protruding from the cutout of his mask, and he had a confident bearing, indicating his position of authority.

"What is this distraction that is keeping you from your stations?" the senior officer barked, annoyed at being pulled away from his other task.

"I'm sorry, sire," one of Riley's captors said. "We found this intruder and weren't sure what to do with her."

The officer peered at Riley for a moment, darting his eyes over her curvy figure bound tightly by her silk robe, then he chuckled dismissively.

"She doesn't look like much of a threat to me," he said, fixing his gaze on Riley's bright green eyes. "Where are you from, young lady?"

"Somewhere far away," Riley said, realizing no one would believe her improbable story of tumbling through time with her unusual time machine.

"And how did you come upon our village of Sparta?" the officer said.

Sparta? Riley thought, widening her eyes. *The famous Greek city-state of ancient legend?*

"I just wandered here in my travels," she said, not sure how to explain her strange circumstances.

The soldier bent down and ran his fingers along the inside of Riley's kimono lapel, rubbing his hand against the silky fabric.

"You certainly don't *look* like you've been traveling very far," he said. "Where did you find this unusual uniform? The fabric isn't like anything I've seen before."

Riley blushed as she felt the tips of his fingers brushing over the side of her breast.

"It comes from a place on the other side of the sea," she said. "It's a bit difficult to explain–"

"Well, you'll have plenty of time to explain later," the officer said. "I'm afraid we'll have to keep you under guard until you can account for your whereabouts. For all we know, you could be a spy for the Persians."

The Persian Army? Riley thought, pinching her eyebrows together. She knew about the countless battles between the Ottoman and Byzantine Empires, but only one between the Persians and Spartans. Could this handsome officer be the famous Greek general, Leonidas, who fought so valiantly to hold off the much larger Arab forces, ultimately succumbing with the rest of his men to their superior numbers?

"Take her to the stockade," he instructed the other soldiers. "But make sure she's well fed and cared for. I'll continue my interrogation after we finish today's training."

"Yes, sire," the other soldiers said, bowing in submission to their superior.

〜

Riley was taken to a stone building with a single locked door and some time later, an attractive woman about ten years her senior appeared at the door, flanked by two guards.

"Are you hungry?" she said, carrying a cistern of water and a brass platter filled with dried meat and fruit.

"Thank you," Riley said, feeling her stomach grumbling from lack of food over the previous twenty-four hours.

"I brought you a *pail*," the woman said, placing an empty bucket beside Riley. "I'm sorry we can't allow you to use the latrines, but perhaps the king will give you more freedom of movement once he ascertains your intentions."

"King *Leonidas*?" Riley said, sitting up suddenly. "The Spartan general?"

"Yes," the woman nodded. "Perhaps you've heard of his exploits. He's never lost a battle."

"No," Riley frowned. "At least not *yet*..."

The woman paused while she studied Riley's face and vestments, unsure what to make of this strange intruder.

"Are you aware of some impending campaign that we don't know of?" she said, peering at Riley's exotic Eastern costume. "You look like you've come from the Orient."

"Perhaps," Riley said, squinting at the woman's linen tunic, trying to guess her position in the village hierarchy. She was eager to gather more information about the precise time in history, wondering if she might be able to assist in the looming battle that changed the course of western civilization.

"Can you stay with me for a while?" she said. "I could use a bit of company in these cramped quarters."

The woman glanced behind her at the soldiers guarding the exit and nodded softly.

"Can we have some privacy?" she said. "It appears our guest may need some extra supervision."

"Of course, Your Majesty," one of the soldiers said, beginning to close the door. "We'll be standing guard outside if you need anything else."

Your Majesty? Riley thought, flaring her eyes. *Could this be Leonidas's wife? She's certainly attractive enough...*

After the soldiers closed the door, the woman sat down cross-legged in front of Riley, peering at her with a soft smile.

"Where exactly are you from?" she said, appraising Riley's milky skin and fair hair. "You don't have the slanted eyes of someone from the Orient."

"America, by way of Japan," Riley nodded, knowing full well no one from the current time would know about these countries.

"I've never heard of those places," the woman said, caressing the lower hem of Riley's robe, humming at the soft feel of the fabric. "It must be awfully far away to have produced such a beautiful garment."

"They are," Riley smiled, feeling her pussy twitching at the flutter of the fabric over her hips from the woman's touch.

"So what brings you so far from home?" the woman said. "You seem like a fish out of water among all these burly warriors dressed up in metal armor."

"I didn't mean to come here particularly," Riley said, fingering her time travel smartphone concealed on the inside pocket of her kimono. "I suppose I just stumbled from one place to another..."

The woman paused while her eyes darted over Riley's colorful robe, noticing her erect nipples darting the soft fabric on the front of her smock.

"You seem remarkably well preserved for someone who's traveled such a long distance..."

"Thank you," Riley said, returning her interest in the pretty queen as she felt a drop of moisture dribbling down the slit of her pussy. "May I ask your name?"

"Dafni," the woman said, holding out her hands with her palms turned upward as a form of welcome.

Riley," Riley nodded, grasping the woman's hands softly.

"Happy to meet you, Riley," Dafni said. "Regardless of your reasons for visiting our village."

"My intentions are purely honorable, I assure you," Riley said, squeezing Dafni's hands gently.

"That's a pity," the queen smiled, squeezing Riley's fingers more firmly. "Because I'm intrigued to see what *other* surprises you've brought with you under that pretty robe of yours."

2

Riley and Dafni's moment of distraction was suddenly interrupted when the heavy door swung open and Leonidas filled the entranceway with his imposing figure.

"Having you been keeping our guest comfortable?" he said, noticing the two women pulling away from one another.

"The best I can, under the circumstances," Dafni frowned, peering around the austere cabin. "It's pretty hard to get comfortable sitting on a pile of hay and using a pot for our waste."

"I suppose you're right about that," Leonidas nodded, smiling at Dafni. "Perhaps we should move to the palace, where we can enjoy some more refreshing provisions?"

"I'm sure Riley would appreciate that," Dafni said. "This is no way to treat our gentle guest."

"Oh?" Leonidas said. "Have you been able to glean more information beyond what she shared during our initial encounter?"

"Only that she comes from somewhere far away. A place

where they seem to treat women like precious commodities."

"I'm sure we can extend Riley a similar measure of respect," Leonidas smiled, pulling his long red cape up over his glistening shoulder. "We're not *all* brutes, interested only in demonstrating our fighting prowess."

Leonidas and Dafni led a train of attendants to a large villa overlooking the valley, then they disappeared into their private quarters while Riley was escorted to an open-air dining room encircled with large marble columns and statues, seated at an oversize table festooned with olives, figs, pomegranates and a multitude of cheeses. When the royal couple reemerged a few minutes later, they were both wearing flowing robes and gold sandals, befitting their station. While the servants continued to arrange the table, Riley noticed the soldiers still standing guard at the corners of the chamber. Whether they were stationed there to protect the king and queen, or to prevent their mysterious guest from slipping away, she couldn't be sure.

"Are you finding these accommodations more to your liking?" Dafni said, noticing Riley peering out over the verdant valley stretching for miles into the distance.

"The *view* is certainly a lot better," Riley smiled.

"Have our servants been attending to your needs?" Leonidas asked.

"I'll say," Riley nodded, taking another bite of a fresh fig. "This gives an entirely new meaning to the concept of a Mediterranean diet."

"A *what*?" Leonidas said, wrinkling his forehead.

"Oh nothing," Riley chuckled. "It's just a term some of my people have given this region of the world."

"Who exactly *are* your people?" Leonidas said, motioning for his staff to leave them alone while they prepared the main course in the kitchen. "You still haven't told me where you come from."

"Somewhere called America," Riley said. "But don't worry, it's well aligned with your interests and values. In fact, our government has adopted your form of democracy and even tried to copy your style of architecture. Greece is the model upon which all of western civilization places its roots."

"You seem quite worldly and knowledgeable for such a young person," Dafni said, biting into a juicy pomegranate as pink juices dribbled down the sides of her cheeks.

"I suppose I've traveled more than most people my age," Riley nodded, suddenly feeling her own juices dribbling down the crack of her ass. "And I'm a keen student of history. I enjoy learning about different cultures."

Leonidas paused as he swirled an olive around in his mouth while his servants laid a freshly roasted pig on a large plate in the center of the table.

"How do you go about traveling from one place to another?" he said, still suspicious about Riley's cryptic back story. "You didn't bring an entourage or any animals as a source of conveyance. And you've packed extremely light for someone who's come such a far distance."

"I'm pretty resourceful," Riley smiling, tapping her smartphone to remind herself that she still carried her emergency exit plan if things went sideways.

"So you're a student of *history*," the king said, pulling off the boar's leg and chomping into it with his bare hands.

"What insights can you share with us from your perspective on the other side of the world?"

"Well, I've studied the numerous wars fought between the armies of the East and the West..."

"You mean the Persians and the Greeks?"

"Among other tribes, yes."

"And what do you make of these never-ending battles? Do you see one side or the other gaining the upper hand at some point in the future?"

"The West will ultimately prevail and prosper in the end," Riley nodded. "But not before thousands more are killed and enslaved on both sides."

"What makes you so sure of the outcome?" Leonidas said, wiping a smear of grease from the side of his mouth. "You sound like the Oracle of Delphi."

"Let's just say I have some special insights from my travels abroad."

"If you have such unique insight, what can you tell us about the *future*? Is there something you can share to help us prepare us for the next incursion?"

Riley paused for a moment, wondering if she'd already gone too far outlining the course of history. She knew that if she revealed too much about the future, that someone in Leonidas's position might be in a position to change it immutably. But there was something about this charismatic leader and his attractive wife that made her want to protect them.

"There's a large army advancing on your location at the present time," she nodded.

Leonidas suddenly stopped chewing, placing his leg bone down slowly on his plate.

"And you know this *how*, exactly?" he said, raising an eyebrow.

"I've traveled far," Riley said. "I have sources of information that you don't have access to."

"If you're so clever," Leonidas smiled uncomfortably. "What is the name of the *general* leading this army?"

"Xerxes," Riley said. "Son of Darius, and current king of the Persian empire."

Leonidas's smirk suddenly evaporated as he slammed his fists down on the table.

"How can you possibly know this, unless you're one of his *spies*?" he shouted. "My scouts have already confirmed the movement of his army, but they assure me it's nothing to worry about. The Aegean Sea is difficult to traverse at this time of year, and our position is ringed with impassable mountains."

"He's also assembling a large *navy* to transport his soldiers. And his army is much larger than your scouts may have led you to believe."

"You're wading into dangerous territory, young lady," Leonidas said, gripping his fists tightly on the table. "These are not accusations you should make lightly."

"Believe me, I'm not making them lightly," Riley said, darting her eyes between the king and queen, who was peering at their young guest with increasing alarm. "I share this information with you only after careful contemplation."

Leonidas paused for an uncomfortably long moment, studying Riley's face while he considered what to do next.

"Exactly how big *is* this army, according to your sources? We have over seven thousand well-armed soldiers, ready to repel anything they throw at us."

"He has over a *hundred thousand* men and eight hundred ships. It will be nearly impossible to stop him."

The general stared back at Riley, tightening his jaw with

every passing second and clasping his hands tighter until his knuckles started to turn blue.

"I will have my scouts redouble their efforts to track Xerxes' army," he said. "If this information proves to be correct, I'll need you to stay here a little longer. You're proving far too valuable as a military aide. Do you have any thoughts on how we might stop his advance?"

"I might," Riley said, remembering how Leonidas had been betrayed at the battle of Thermopylae and how his army was outflanked and subsequently annihilated when they were overrun by the opposing army. "But it will require your changing your battle strategy and preparing some new tools of war."

Leonidas glanced briefly in the direction of his wife, not noticing the darting of her robe from her erect nipples, as Dafni had become increasingly aroused listening to their attractive and brazen young guest.

"You're just *full* of surprises today, aren't you?" Leonidas said, staring back at Riley like she'd just predicted his untimely end.

Which, unbeknownst to him, she had. But luckily for Leonidas, her engineering training and knowledge of modern chemistry might be the one thing separating him and the rest of his settlement from complete obliteration.

3

———————

After they finished their meal, Leonidas instructed his wife to settle Riley in one of the palace's guest rooms while he attended to other business. Riley was escorted to a large bedchamber with a steep drop to the valley, then the queen left her with a change of clothes, posting two guards outside her door. A few minutes later, some attendants entered the room with buckets of hot water, filling her large bathtub overlooking the canyon. Riley took off her robe and hid her time machine, then she slipped into the warm bath, purring at the sublime feeling of the warm water lapping at her bare skin. Sometime later, there was a knock at the door and Riley sat up, covering her breasts instinctively.

"Yes?" she called from her tub, not wanting to get out of her comfortable cocoon.

"It's Dafni," the queen said from the other side of the door. "Do you have everything you need? Is there anything else I can bring for you?"

Riley paused for a moment, feeling her pussy fluttering

while she remembered the way Dafni had peered at her in the stockade and at dinner.

"I'm having a bath now," she said, secretly wishing the queen would join her.

"How's your water temperature?" Dafni said. "Shall I have the attendants bring you more hot water?"

"If it's not too much trouble," Riley said, feeling the chill of the night air spilling through her open bedroom window.

A few moments later, a retinue of servants carried some pails of hot water into Riley's room, followed closely behind by the queen.

"You may leave us now," she said, waving her hand at the attendants.

After they left the room, she dipped her hand into Riley's bath water and nodded her head softly, peering at the girl's bare shoulders peeking above the surface.

"It's a bit cool," she said, lifting up one of the pails and pouring it slowly into the opposite end of the tub near Riley's feet.

"Mmm, that's much better," Riley nodded, closing her eyes and flapping her legs slowly under the bubbling water.

"Is there anything else I can do to make you feel comfortable?" the queen said, running her fingers tantalizingly over the surface of the water. "Is the tub large enough for your liking?"

"It's bigger than I'm accustomed to back home," Riley said, feeling her pussy twitching as the swirling water circulated around her hips. "It's a pity it's being wasted on only one person..."

Dafni raised up on her knees and arched her back to display her firm breasts pressing against her soft tunic.

"Would you like some company?" she said.

"If you're not too busy," Riley smiled. "That is, if your husband doesn't need your attention–"

"He's too busy conferring with his war council," Dafni said. "You really put a burr under his ass with all that talk of the Persians marching toward our territory."

"Sorry," Riley nodded. "I figured he'd want to know about his enemy's plans as soon as possible."

"Yes," Dafni said, pulling off her robe and placing it on the side of Riley's bed next to her kimono. "Although I'm not sure how he's going to fight off an army more than ten times his size."

"Leave that to me," Riley said, peering up at Dafni's hourglass figure as she dipped a toe into the water at the opposite end of the tub. "I've got a few ideas how he might be able to use your unique topography to your advantage."

"Speaking of *topography*," the queen said, watching the waves splash over Riley's erect nipples as she lowered herself into the water. "Yours is even more beautiful than I imagined watching you wrapped up in that exotic Eastern costume."

"Yours too," Riley said, spreading her knees apart to accommodate the queen's hips resting against the opposite side of the tub. "It seems the two of us had other things on our mind over dinner than preparing for battle."

"Although I *was* considering a different type of full-body contact..." Dafni smiled, tilting her body forward and kissing Riley softly on her lips.

"Mmm," Riley purred, feeling the queen's bare tits rubbing up against hers in the swirling water. "It's been a while since I felt the touch of another woman..."

"Do you prefer it over that of a *man*?" Dafni said, reaching under the water to caress Riley's breasts with her two hands.

"I like it both ways," Riley nodded, bending her knees and shifting her hips forward until her pussy pressed up against the queen's. "There's a time and a place for a man's hard cock *and* for a woman's soft pussy. It just depends on the mood I'm in."

"I feel the same way," the queen said, slipping her tongue into Riley's mouth as the two women began to rock their hips together.

"Oh?" Riley panted, groaning into the queen's mouth. "The king doesn't mind you dabbling when he's not looking?"

"He has enough of his *own* private liaisons," Dafni smiled. "It's become part of our routine, to keep our marriage from becoming stale. Sometimes we even invite our partners into our bedroom, to share the spoils."

"That sounds like fun," Riley said, humping her hips harder against Dafni's pussy as the water in the tub began to slosh around and spill over the edges. "Though I don't imagine he trusts me enough to invite him into his bedroom yet."

"Let me take care of that," the queen smiled, wrapping her arms around Riley's back and grinding her pussy harder against Riley's slippery slit. "But not until I've had my fill of your pretty body first."

"Yes," Riley huffed, feeling her orgasm welling up inside her. "You feel exquisite."

"Come with me," Dafni grunted as her pupils began to dilate. "Hold me while we share the pleasure together."

"Oh my God," Riley groaned, feeling herself passing over the tipping point. *"Gahhh!"*

"Mmmft," the queen hissed, moaning simultaneously into Riley's mouth.

While the two women held onto each other tightly, jerking and shaking their bodies together in the roiling bath water, suddenly the prospect of a brutal land battle pitting the forces of the two greatest military powers of their era together, seemed a million miles away.

4

———

The following morning, Leonidas invited Riley to join him and his wife for breakfast on their terrace overlooking the valley. Whether he knew about the two women's brief affair in Riley's bathtub the previous night, Riley couldn't be sure. But judging by the way Dafni looked at her young courtesan, it was obvious the queen still had designs on the mysterious interloper. After the servants prepared the breakfast spread, Leonidas raised his glass of wine in recognition of Riley.

"My scouts have confirmed your assessment of Xerxes' movement," he said. "It appears their army is much larger than originally considered. Our spies indicate that he's planning to attack from the north, through the narrow pass of Thermopylae, with a simultaneous naval assault at Artemisium, south of Athens."

"What is your plan to repel them?" Riley nodded, already familiar with the famous story of Leonidas's doomed campaign to fend off the giant army.

"The pass is extremely narrow," Leonidas said. "Their

advantage in manpower will be neutralized once it's compressed to face our soldiers. Our phalanx should be able to resist their advance when we're fighting them one-on-one."

"Isn't there another route around the mountain?" Riley said, remembering the way one of the local residents had betrayed Leonidas by revealing to the Persians the secret route to outflank him. "If Xerxes surrounds you on two sides, you'll have no way of escaping."

"We'll post guards along the alternate path and position a reserve force to repel them," Leonidas nodded, confident of the infallibility of his plan.

Riley paused for a long moment while she peered at Dafni and the king with a worried expression.

"You don't seem convinced of the soundness of our plan," Leonidas said, placing his goblet on the table as he studied the young girl's countenance.

"You'll be outnumbered twenty to one," Riley said. "You might be able to hold them off temporarily at the pass, but your divided army won't be able to stop them from circum-navigating you on two sides."

Leonidas hesitated as his muscular chest expanded and contracted from his obvious irritation at Riley's assessment of his plan.

"What do you propose?" he said, clenching his fists slowly beside his place setting. "You seem to have exceptional military insight for someone so young and inexperienced."

Riley paused once again while she evaluated the modern military options.

"What if you lure his army deeper into the pass and try to trap his forces from opposite sides?"

"But you said yourself that our numbers would be insufficient to hold them off for long. How will we keep them from overrunning our smaller position?"

"You won't need to if you can make the mountain fall on top of them."

Leonidas laughed while he glanced at his wife with a dismissive expression.

"First you pretend to be the Oracle of Delphi, and now you feign to have the powers of the great god *Zeus*, himself?"

"Hear her out, Leo," the queen said, peering at Riley. "She proved to be right about her foreknowledge of Xerxes' plans. Maybe she brings some other useful knowledge from the faraway lands from where she came."

"I'm all ears," Leonidas said, relaxing his grip and placing his utensils on his plate. "If you can find a way to move a *mountain*, I'll never doubt your abilities again."

Riley peered down toward the courtyard, noticing a thin tendril of smoke rising from a simmering fire containing charred logs in the pit.

"Thermopylae means *hot gates*, doesn't it?" she said.

"Yes," Leonidas said. "From the smoldering springs in the area."

"Those springs are heated from a substance called sulfur," Riley nodded. "If you can bring me enough of that water, I can boil off the residue and make a compound that will make Zeus's thunderbolts look like child's play. The resulting explosion will break the mountain apart and bury Xerxes' troops in their tracks."

"That's a pretty fantastic story," Leonidas said, raising his eyebrows. "But you'd have to show me a *demonstration* before I committed my forces to such a vulnerable position."

"How soon can you bring me the sulfuric water?" Riley said. "It will take a few days to prepare the formula."

"Two or three days perhaps, by horseback," he said.

"And how long do your scouts say it will be before Xerxes' forces cross the Aegean?"

"Maybe a week or so," Leonidas nodded. "But how will our Athenian allies stop their *navy*? Themistocles has only a few hundred triremes, and the Persian fleet outnumbers his three to one."

Riley peered up at a lantern at the side of the terrace, noticing it was burning some kind of oil in a pot.

"By deploying *another* weapon not yet invented," she smiled. "It will require a slightly different composition of materials, but if we work quickly, we can create something that will send the Persians fleeing in terror: Greek Fire."

"We've used flaming arrows before," Leonidas said. "They're not very effective, since they can be quickly doused and difficult to fire in close quarters."

"This fire will be *sprayed* onto your opponent using a liquid propellant," Riley nodded. "And by using pine resin as a catalyst, it will be difficult to remove from their bodies and extinguish."

"You're just *full* of surprises, aren't you, young lady?" Leonidas said, leaning back in his chair and steepling his fingers over his chest, suddenly feeling more confident in his ability to fend off the invading Persians.

"You have no idea," Dafni smiled, winking at Riley from the other side of the table.

5

Over the next few days, Riley and Leonidas's men worked diligently to prepare the new weapons of war. It took some time to source the materials, since both the improvised TNT and the liquid naphtha required a complex mixture of compounds not readily available in the southern regions of ancient Greece. Fortunately, Riley's engineering studies at MIT had equipped her with the basic knowledge to prepare and mix the necessary compounds to create the explosive devices that wouldn't be invented for another millennium.

The hardest part was creating the quicklime needed to mix with the sulfur and crude oil used to heat their lamps, in order to create the flammable mixture that would become known as Greek Fire. Riley didn't feel too conflicted about introducing this modern technology before its time, since the Greeks would eventually decipher how to make a similar concoction and use it to protect their empire for many centuries. With the formula closely guarded within the royal households of the Byzantine kings, the secret never escaped into the wild and was never used outside the frequent clashes between the Ottomans and the Greeks.

Instead of being mined from limestone, Riley had to arrange for the collection of huge quantities of seashells, which were then super-heated in a stone furnace to separate the CO_2 from the shells' calcium carbonate to extract the volatile calcium oxide. Once the quicklime mixture was liberated, it was a fairly simple process of mixing it with the purified sulfur, distilled naphtha, and boiled pine resin to create the sticky and super-flammable cocktail that would terrorize the Persians and Ottomans for centuries. Once enough of the mixture had been stored in large clay pots, Riley was ready to demonstrate the power of this new invention.

"How's your cooking coming along?" Leonidas said, pacing impatiently among the many soldiers Riley had diverted to attend to each of the tasks. "Is it almost ready to serve to our enemy?"

"I think so," Riley nodded. "But we're going to have to be careful about how we ignite it so as not to risk injury to your soldiers."

"What exactly did you have in mind?" Leonidas said, twisting his nose while he whiffed the noxious cocktail swirling in the open caldrons.

"I've got a couple of ideas," Riley said, peering at some of the small clay pots decorating the front of palace gardens. "Do you have some fresh mortar we can use to fuse together those pots?"

"My masons are building an addition to the palace in the east wing," Leonidas nodded. "But why do you want to fuse them together?"

"We're going to make a type of *grenade* to hold the liquid, which you can hurl at the invaders when they get close enough."

"But how will you make them *explode*?"

"If you can get your men to prepare a few of the devices with a little hole in the top, I'll show you in a few minutes," Riley said.

"I sure hope you know what you're doing," Leonidas huffed, instructing one of his lieutenants to supervise the process.

"I thought you said you weren't going to doubt me again?" Riley smiled.

"That was *after* you demonstrated the effectiveness of these magical weapons," he said, allowing a small grin to form on one side of his mouth.

"Never fear, my king," Riley nodded, glancing at his washboard abs, glistening in the afternoon sun. "I'll put on a fireworks show like you've never seen, soon enough."

After a few of the small pots were assembled and allowed to set, Riley picked one of them up and dipped a cup into the nearest naphtha vat, carefully emptying its contents into the small hole left on the lid of the pot. Then she inserted a short wick into an improvised plug and pushed it into the hole to keep the volatile liquid from leaking out.

"Can I trouble you for a light?" she said, peering at Leonidas.

"A *what*?" the general said, wrinkling his forehead.

"A torch, a candle, anything with a small flame."

"Of course," Leonidas said, motioning for one of his attendants to fetch a smoldering log from a nearby fire.

When he handed it to Riley, she held the torch in one hand and the improvised bomb far away in her outstretched arm.

"You might want to have your men stand back a little further," she said, noticing some of the soldiers creeping closer, curious to see how this new device was going to work. "It's going to produce quite a bang."

"Um, sure..." Leonidas said, motioning with his hand for his troop to withdraw a few paces.

Riley peered about the courtyard for a suitable target for her demonstration, settling on a crumbling structure with a collapsed roof.

"Do you use that building for anything?" she said to the general.

"It's just an old storehouse for grain," he said. "We haven't used it for quite some time."

"Good," she said, drawing the flame closer to the wick atop the clay pot. "Watch out for flying debris–"

"Flying *what*...?" the king said, pinching his eyebrows.

Riley lifted the burning log over the wick of the pot, then she hurled it toward the base of the crumbling building. When the pot struck the wall, it erupted in a giant explosion, sending shards of broken pottery in every direction with a large fireball above the base of the smoldering structure. When the smoke cleared, Leonidas's eyes widened when he saw that the building had been blown completely apart.

"By the gods of Olympia!" he exclaimed, hardly believing his eyes. "How did you do that?"

"With a little help from modern science and earth's natural resources," she smiled. "You just need to know how to mix the proper ratio of ingredients."

Leonidas paused for a moment as he surveyed the conflagration in the courtyard.

"I wouldn't want this knowledge falling into the enemy's hands," he nodded. "Can you provide me with the instructions so I can make *more* of it when needed?"

"Of course," Riley said. "But I recommend you share the process with one trusted craftsman and have him pass this on within his family to keep the secret safe for future generations. This technology can change the entire shape of world if it gets out into the wild."

"I'm way ahead of you," Leonidas said, motioning for one of his attendants to work closely with Riley.

"Good," Riley said, smelling the odor of the reeking chemicals permeating her new clothes. "Do you mind if I take some time to clean up before we continue preparing the rest of the weapons?"

"You certainly deserve a break after all you've done," Leonidas nodded. "But don't go too far. I'm eager to see you demonstrate this *other* invention that can allegedly move mountains."

"I won't be long," Riley smiled, noticing Dafni leaning over the railing of their terrace, monitoring the developments in the courtyard with keen interest. "I'll be making the earth move soon enough..."

6

───────────

When Riley returned to the palace, the queen was waiting for her at the top of the stairs, peering at her with a broad smile.

"That was pretty impressive," she said, noticing the stains on Riley's smock from her handling of the dirty chemicals. "When I saw that explosion, I almost climaxed myself. If you weren't so soiled from all those smelly chemicals, I'd fuck you where you stand."

"It shouldn't take long to clean myself up," Riley smiled, happy to see the queen was thinking the same thing she was. "That is, if you don't mind having your servants prepare my bath once again..."

"No worries," Dafni said, summoning one of her attendants. "This time, I'm going to clean you *myself*. I've been dreaming of all the ways I can ravage you once I get you out of that tub."

"Sounds delicious," Riley grinned, feeling her pussy twitching at the thought of getting the queen alone on her kingsize bed. "Let me get out of these sweaty clothes and wash this smelly stuff off my body. There's a *different* kind of bouquet I'd prefer to inhale for the rest of the afternoon."

"I'm willing to share as soon as you're able," the queen said, grabbing Riley's hand and pulling her toward the guest bedroom.

When they entered Riley's chamber, the tub had already been filled, and Dafni wasted no time tearing off Riley's soiled clothing and lowering her into the water as she kneeled behind her at the head of the basin.

"Mmm, that feels heavenly," Riley purred as the queen rolled a soft sea sponge over her tingling skin.

"Yes," Dafni smiled, watching the water slosh over Riley's firm breasts and hard nipples. "And it looks just as glorious as it must feel. You must have been dying to get out of that baking sun all morning."

"Well, I have to admit that I was dreaming about a *different* kind of explosion once I finished my work in the courtyard," Riley grinned, raising her hips out of the water as Dafni's washcloth slipped between her legs.

"You're beautiful," the queen said, staring at Riley's bald mound. "Do *all* women in America clip their pubic hair like you do?"

"The modern-day ones, yes," Riley nodded, moaning as Dafni's sponge slid over her dripping snatch.

"I like it," the queen smiled, kissing the back of Riley's neck while she rolled her hand between the girl's thighs. "It will make it easier for me to *lick* you down there when we get out of the tub."

"It feels even better when you rub other things against your naked vulva. Perhaps I can groom your lower regions once I'm finished in the bath. It's a singular pleasure rubbing two shaved pussies together."

"That sounds incredibly decadent," Dafni groaned, rocking her hips unconsciously behind Riley's head. "I can't wait–"

"It's your turn then," Riley said, lifting herself out of the bathtub and turning around to remove the queen's clothing. "Do you have a sharp blade and some lather for removing your hair? I'd love to do the honors..."

Dafni scooted out of the bedroom and returned a few moments later with a sharp carving knife and a foaming soap bar from her bedroom.

"I'm not exactly sure this will work," she said, staring at Riley with trembling hands. "I don't know if I'm ready to have you swiping this so close to my sensitive parts–"

"Leave that to me," Riley smiled, helping Dafni step into the tub. "I've had a little practice with this sort of thing."

Riley positioned the queen's hips on the top edge of the tub, then she kneeled between her legs, slowly separating her thighs.

"It might be better if you close your eyes while I do this," she said, positioning the edge of the blade just above the top of her curly fringe. "It will *feel* a little less scary than it looks."

Dafni peered down at Riley holding the blade over her quivering abdomen, then she took a deep breath.

"We've trusted you this far and you haven't disappointed us," she said, tilting her head backwards and closing her eyes. "Just be careful not to slice off any of the *important* parts."

"I wouldn't dream of it," Riley smiled, rubbing some of the foam into the queen's bush and scraping the knife slowly over the top of her pubis.

The blade made a scraping noise as it began clipping her hair from its roots, and Riley splashed some warm water between the queen's legs to remove the clippings while she panted the closer Riley's knife got to the top of her folds. But the girl was careful to slow her movement and hold the knife perpendicular to the surface of her skin, being cautious not to nick the queen or cause her any injury.

"I've never felt this vulnerable with anyone before," she said as Riley scratched away the few remaining hairs at the base of her pubis and around the sides of her hardening clit. "There's something about you that makes me trust you unconditionally."

"Not even with your *husband*?" Riley smiled, swiping away the last of the loose strands.

"He's seen me like this, of course," Dafni nodded, tilting her head up and peering down at Riley's handiwork. "But never holding sharp objects."

"That's too bad," Riley said, watching the queen's juices dripping down the slit in the middle of her shaved vulva. "Because he's pretty *hot* dressed up in his battle gear with his big sword resting beside his hips."

"I prefer to make use of his *other* sword," Dafni smiled. "He's quite adept at using both of them in the right circumstances."

"I can imagine," Riley said, moving her face closer to Dafni's shaved snatch to inspect her work. "He seems larger than life in more ways than one."

"I think he fancies you," the queen nodded, spreading her legs further apart and tilting her hips upward to meet Riley's face. "I imagine he'd be pretty excited to have *two* bare pussies distract him from his war preparations."

"We'll have to see if we can tear him away," Riley said. "I'd hate to miss my chance if our plans go astray..."

"You better not let it," Dafni said, clutching the back of Riley's head and pulling her face hard into her dripping crotch. "Because I've been having way too many fantasies about how much the three of us can enjoy our newfound freedom once we win the battle."

"Mmm," Riley nodded, pressing her tongue into the queen's slit and sliding it upward until it reached the top of her folds. She pursed her lips and encircled her flaring bud, then she reached behind the queen's ass and pulled her hips harder toward her, sucking her jewel into her mouth.

"Oh *fuck*," Dafni hissed, watching Riley eating her freshly shaved pussy. "This feels even better without all the unnecessary decoration. You weren't kidding about how good this feels."

"Do you like the *view* better, too?" Riley said, pulling her face away from the queen's dripping snatch momentarily.

Dafni peered between her legs at her pink folds, noticing her erect clit sticking out like a ripe cherry on a tree.

"God damn, that's sexy," she grunted, drifting her hands between her legs and caressing her soft folds. "And it *feels* a lot better, too."

"Why don't we try rubbing something *else* against your bare skin?" Riley smiled, pushing the queen's hands away from her throbbing crotch. "We've only begun to scratch the surface of the possibilities here..."

"You mean–?" Dafni said as Riley slowly raised her body out of the bath water.

"Exactly," Riley said, stepping out of the tub and clasping the queen's hand while she pulled their dripping bodies toward the bed.

They flopped onto the mattress then Dafni rolled on top of Riley, grinding her hips against the younger girl, groaning at the sensation of their smooth pussies rubbing together.

"You have no idea how much I've dreamt of this

moment," the queen said, sitting up and kneeling between Riley's thighs as she pulled one of her legs upwards. "But now that you can see me in all my glory, I want you even more..."

Dafni rammed her pussy between Riley's splayed legs and began grinding their bare vulvas together, clasping Riley's upturned leg against her shaking tits as she arched her head upward, rolling her eyes in delirious pleasure.

"Yes, *fuck me,* Dafni," Riley grunted, rocking her hips equally hard against the queen's flapping hips. "I can feel *every* part of you–"

"I'm going to come so hard against your pretty pussy," Dafni moaned, digging her fingernails into the back of Riley's upturned thigh.

"Oh God, that feels so good–" Riley groaned, grabbing the sides of Dafni's buttocks as she felt her floodgates begin to unlock.

When she began gushing against Dafni's flapping legs, the queen wailed at the top of her lungs, pressing her pussy hard against Riley's spurting slit, blinking her eyes as their combined juices squirted in every direction. After what seemed like an eternity squealing in each other's embrace, they heard a strange sound coming from the direction of Riley's bedroom door, and they turned their heads to see Leonidas standing with his legs apart and his huge cock pointing straight up between the flaps of his leather battle skirt.

"It *took* you long enough," Dafni smiled, rolling off Riley and flopping onto the bed beside her, exposing their two glistening pussies. "Were you planning on coming over here and sharing in the spoils?"

"I suppose I can pull myself away for a few moments," he

grinned, unfastening his tunic to reveal his magnificently toned body. "Thanks to Riley, we've got someone else who can supervise the workers in my absence."

"Thank heavens," Riley sighed. "I was beginning to think you were only a *fighter*, not a lover."

7

Leonidas walked over to the end of the bed, peering at the two women's shaved pussies while his big pole bounced up and down excitedly.

"Is this another strange custom where you come from?" he said, darting his eyes across their glistening vulvas. "You don't like the natural adornment of your feminine areas?"

"It's not so much *that*," Riley said. "It's more about minimizing the interference from all the scratchy hairs so our partners can enjoy our flowers without any distraction."

"Plus, you get to appreciate our girly parts in all their natural glory," the queen smiled. "I know how much you Greek men idolize youthful beauty."

"It *does* take me back to my adolescent days," Leonidas nodded as a thick string of pre-cum dripped from the tip of his bobbing organ.

"Go ahead," the queen grinned, spreading her legs further apart. "Why don't you try a little sample for yourself? I think you'll find it especially *tasty*."

"Mmm," Leonidas nodded as he dropped down onto his

knees in front of his wife's dripping slit. "You know how much I love to lick your kolpos."

"Yes," Dafni moaned when her husband buried his head in her pink folds. "Suck my smooth pussy. Taste my sweet cherry..."

"Mhhh," the king hummed as he gripped his wife's hips with both hands, pulling her harder toward him.

Meanwhile, Riley couldn't resist turning toward Dafni while they rubbed their tits together as the queen moaned into her mouth.

"God, that feels good," the queen groaned. "Climb on top of me and rub your pussy against my shaved pubis so my husband can taste *both* of us."

Riley didn't waste any time rolling on top of Dafni and pressing their hips together while she undulated her ass inches away from the king's flaring eyes.

"Do you *like* that, sweetheart?" Dafni panted. "Are you enjoying staring at two shaved pussies this close up?"

"Fuck yes," Leonidas grunted, lifting his head while he watched the two women grinding their mounds together.

"Go ahead," Dafni said. "Lick both of us. I'm sure Riley won't mind—"

"*Hell* no," Riley huffed as she tilted her hips toward the queen's splayed legs, rubbing their swollen glands together. "I've wanted to fuck your husband pretty much from the moment I landed in your dusty courtyard. Having the *three* of you together is a dream come true."

"Damn, that's a pretty sight," Leonidas said, sticking out his tongue and sliding it between their joined slits like a kid licking a double-scoop ice cream cone. "You weren't kidding how much better this feels without any hairs in the way."

Dafni raised her head for a few moments to peer at the

sight of her husband lapping up the scent of the two women's juices dripping between their connected vulvas.

"I imagine it would feel even *better* sliding your *cock* between our bare pussies," she grunted, rocking her hips harder against Riley's undulating hips. "Why don't you take turns fucking our pussies while we rub our mounds together? Feeling your big spear inside us will be the icing on the cake."

Leonidas pulled away from licking the women's two slits and he stood up, swinging his cock from side to side while he slapped his thick organ against the sides of Riley's ass, then he slowly slid it down the crack of her ass until he found her dripping hole. He pinched the tip of his pole with two fingers to position it against her opening then he rammed his hips hard against her ass, sinking the full length of his erection into her slurping tunnel in one quick movement.

"Unghh," Riley grunted when she felt his thick organ pounding against the end of her cavity.

She pressed her lips hard against Dafni, slipping her tongue deep inside her mouth while Leonidas slammed his hips against her ass, rocking both of the women hard against the shaking bed.

"Oh my God," she exclaimed, staring into Dafni's eyes. "He's *huge!*"

"There's more than *one* reason why he's the leader of our settlement," the queen nodded. "Besides being the best swordsman, he's also the most adept at using his other natural endowments."

Riley raised her head, peering at Dafni with a deep flush on her face.

"I'm going to come," she panted. "I can't hold it any longer..."

"I'm right behind you, sweetie," Dafni groaned as she dug her fingernails into Riley's back. "Keep rubbing your pussy against me. I can feel Leo's balls tightening–"

"Oh fuck," Leonidas growled, slapping his hips harder against Riley's ass while he watched the two women kissing passionately. "This is incredible. *Gahhhh!*"

While he slammed his pole as far into Riley's pulsating pussy as he could, Riley erupted her juices against his testicles, gushing over his balls onto Dafni's slit, spraying their combined juices over each other's asses while the three lovers held onto each other tightly. When they finally finished shaking in mutual ecstasy, Leonidas flopped down beside the two women with his thick organ dripping streams of cum down the underside of his upturned shaft.

Dafni took one look at his leaking cock then she rolled off Riley, sliding over to the other side of her husband.

"Whatever happened to sharing the spoils?" she said. "I thought you were going to take *turns* fucking the two of us?"

"I'm sorry, sweetheart," Leonidas frowned. "I guess I got a little carried away watching the two of you rubbing your pussies together. It was kind of hard to resist climaxing at the sight of your beautiful asses grinding together."

"That's okay," Dafni grinned, noticing her husband's dick still pointing straight up and bouncing over his flexing abdominal muscles. "I can think of another way we can rub our bodies together while sharing you between the two of us. That is, if you think you can stay hard for a little longer..."

"Are you *kidding* me?" Leonidas smiled. "I haven't been this turned on since I was fourteen years old. I could probably stay hard all afternoon watching the two of you."

"Good," the queen said, lifting herself up on her knees and straddling the king's hips with his cock flapping against her smooth belly. "We're going to fuck you from opposite sides this time. What do you say, Riley? Do you want to be in the driver's seat this time?"

"You mean, on *top*, facing each other while we rub our pussies together with his cock resting between us?" Riley said, flaring her eyes.

"Exactly," Dafni nodded. "That way, we can squirt our juices over his burning balls while he squirts his cum over our shaved mounds."

"That sounds *hot*," Riley said, hopping up onto the king's stomach and turning to face Dafni as she flexed her buttocks over his thick tufts of pubic hair.

When he felt the two women's slits pressing together against his shaft and beginning to rock their hips up and down, Leonidas dropped his head back onto the mattress, groaning in delirious pleasure.

"Oh my God," he groaned. "Just when I thought this couldn't get any better. Your bodies look like Greek sculptures resting atop my cock..."

"You're not the *only* one who's got an amazing view," Dafni panted as she peered down between the two women's bouncing tits at Leonidas's long shaft sliding up and down between their glistening bellies. "Come on our *tits* this time while we squirt our juices over your balls."

"Fuck, yes," Leonidas huffed, watching the two women humping their hips rapidly against his upturned erection as he felt his balls beginning to tighten once again. "I'm going to come like Mount Vesuvius."

When Dafni and Riley saw him spurting thick ropes of cum up between their breasts, they pressed their pussies harder against his erupting organ, groaning together as their juices began squirting over their asses and the king's balls. It was a feast for the senses while they shook their bodies together, feeling the shared pleasure of their bodies releasing their pent-up excitement while they smelled the fragrant scent of their sexual juices commingling and listened to the symphony of their combined voices groaning together in mutual harmony.

8

"Wow," Leonidas panted when he came down from his powerful climax. "That's going to be pretty hard to beat. I haven't come that hard in a long time."

"Well, if you're looking for an even bigger bang," Riley huffed. "We still haven't tested my *other* explosive invention yet..."

"You mean the one that can supposedly move mountains?" the king said.

"Among other things," Riley nodded.

"We better get back at it then," Leonidas said, rolling off the bed and strapping on his battle fatigues. "I'd almost forgotten we have a huge army marching toward our position."

"We're going to need some slightly different ingredients this time," Riley said, sponging off her sticky skin and draping a loose tunic over her naked body.

"What *now*?" the king said, squinting back at her. "Ground-up whale bones and fried bull testicles?"

"Not quite so exotic," Riley chuckled. "We're going to need a lot of *shit*. Piles and piles of hot, steaming shit."

"Whatever are you going to use *that* for?" Leonidas said, twisting his face into a curious frown.

"Feces contains something especially useful," Riley nodded. "A chemical called nitrogen. Besides being incredibly explosive once properly extracted, it's what makes your crops grow so much better after they're fertilized."

"Well, we certainly have an abundance of dung behind our latrines and in our horse stables. Exactly how much are you going to need?"

"As much as you can scare up," Riley said, strapping on her sandals as the queen wrinkled her forehead at her strange chemistry lesson. "And we're going to need to collect it in a large open pit."

"I'm not sure the citizens of Sparta are going to be happy about that," the king said. "There's a reason our outhouses are located some distance away from everyone's homes."

"Hopefully, they won't have to tolerate the odor for too long," Riley said. "It should only take a couple of days to extract the necessary ingredients."

"What else are you going to need?" Leonidas huffed. "Do you want us to collect our *piss* in a pot, also?"

"Actually," Riley grinned. "Urine is a helpful catalyst for extracting the nitrates from manure. Be we can save that until later. The other things we're going to need are some black coal and plenty of lamp oil."

Leonidas chuckled as he strapped on his breastplate and pulled his ornamental helmet over his head.

"From pretty pussies to smelly waste pits," he said. "You sure know how to change the mood pretty quickly."

"Alchemy can be a messy business, just like good sex,"

Riley smiled. "But I assure you that in the end, the results will be equally satisfying."

When Riley and Leonidas returned to the courtyard, the general set about instructing his men to collect the necessary ingredients for Riley's improvised explosive, having his newly appointed aide follow them around to take notes on the mixing of the ingredients. After all the manure had been dug up and placed in a large open pit, Leonidas was relieved when Riley instructed for the mixture to be covered with wood ash and straw to begin aerating the material.

"What now?" he said, staring at the smelly pit.

"Now's the time to add urine," Riley nodded matter-of-factly.

"You're going to mix urine with *shit*?" Leonidas said, shaking his head. "I've never heard of such a crazy idea."

"Neither have your enemies," Riley said, glancing at his aide while the man took detailed notes. "That's why you need to keep it a closely guarded secret."

"And how exactly do you plan on *mixing* the urine with this fetid cocktail?"

"The old-fashioned way," Riley smiled. "By unzipping your pants and relieving yourself the way everybody else does."

Leonidas pulled his head back, flaring his eyes in surprise.

"You want my men to piss openly all over this strange concoction?" he said.

"Mm-hmm," Riley nodded. "The two ingredients will

combine to create a volatile mixture once they start to decompose."

"And how long will all of this *take*?" the general said, beginning to become impatient at Riley's wild concoctions.

"A couple of days, give or take," she said. "Assuming it's stirred sufficiently."

"Stirred?" the king said, staring at Riley, dumbfounded. "You mean, somebody's got to go in there and–"

"Uh-huh," she nodded. "The more the merrier. The faster we aerate the mixture, the sooner the nitrogen can be separated."

"I sure hope you know what you're doing," Leonidas sighed, instructing his aide to begin organizing his men for the unpleasant task. "I need my soldiers to be focused on preparing for the upcoming battle instead of wading through shit. This isn't exactly what they signed up for when they joined the army."

"It'll be worth it in the end," Riley smiled. "In a few short days, we'll be able to give them an even more convincing demonstration of the power of modern chemistry. Once they see what this new powder can do, it will silence any of their reservations about preparing these new weapons of war."

9

———

Over the next couple of days, Riley watched bemused while Leonidas's soldiers one-by-one unzipped their pants and held onto their streaming peckers while they emptied their bladders into the fetid pit and alternated wading into the bed to stir the mixture as the fluids slowly began to evaporate and the black mixture started to turn white. After it turned to a salty, granular mixture, she had the residue emptied into large clay pots, after which she added a precise mixture of distilled candle oil, crushed charcoal, and sulphur.

"It's turned *black* again," Leonidas said, sticking his head over one of the pots and smelling the strong scent of crude TNT. "Is that a good sign?"

"It is indeed," Riley nodded, looking around for another target of her next demonstration. "I'm almost ready to give this a try. But we're going to need a sturdier object to test the explosion..."

"You mean a sturdier *building*? I'm not sure I like the idea of blowing up somebody's house–"

"I was thinking of something a little more *solid*," Riley

said, peering up at a nearby embankment on the edge of the settlement. "Can you have your men dig a ten-foot-deep pit on the crest of that hill?"

"I suppose so," Leonidas said, motioning for his aide. "After wading through a foul mix of shit and piss for the last couple of days, digging a hole in the ground will seem like a walk in the park. What exactly do you propose to do with it?"

"We're going to fill it with some of this powder," Riley nodded. "You're about to see what the Chinese invented hundreds of years before gunpowder and TNT found its way to the West."

"I can't wait to see *this* one," the king nodded. "If it burns even *half* as hard as it took to make this strange cocktail, it should be quite a show."

"I assure you, my king," Riley smiled. "This explosion will knock your socks off like nothing you've ever experienced."

After Leonidas's men filled the hole with a few shovels-full of the black powder, Riley instructed them to place a long strand of cloth soaked in naphtha into the mixture and trace it down the side of the hill toward the waiting general.

"Do you want to do the honors this time?" she said, placing a burning log near the end of the fuse.

"You want *me* to light the wick this time?" the king said.

"You and your men are going to have to do it soon enough," Riley nodded. "In the heat of battle, they'll need to light the fuses quickly to ignite both weapons at the appropriate moments."

"Alright," Leonidas said, moving the flame closer to the end of the string.

Riley glanced around her, noticing his soldiers staring up from the base of the hill, wondering what the strange girl from the East had cooked up this time

"Before you set it off," she said, raising her hand. "You better have your men shift to the side of the embankment instead of standing directly underneath it. I'm afraid this might create a bit of a landslide."

The general paused while he instructed his men to divide into two groups.

"Move back a few hundred meters on opposite sides of the hill," he directed. "And keep your shields in front of your bodies in case of flying debris. This time, the pieces might be a little bigger."

The men shifted further to the sides of the embankment, then they crouched down onto their knees with their heavy shields covering their bodies like they'd been trained to do in their famous phalanx formation. After Leonidas saw that everyone was ready, he held the flame to the end of the wick, then he watched the fuse crackle and spark while the thin trail of fire ascended the embankment. When it crested the hill and disappeared out of view, he peered at Riley with a puzzled expression, waiting for the big bang she'd promised.

"I thought you said this was going to be an even bigger explosion than the last one," he said, squinting at her.

"It will," Riley said, motioning for him to take cover as she crouched next to him behind his shield while they peered up at the tendril of smoke disappearing into the newly dug hole.

Suddenly, there was an enormous explosion as the top of the mountain erupted in a giant fireball and huge rocks began pouring down into the courtyard, rolling dangerously close to the shaking soldiers hiding behind their shields. The shaking of the earth continued for well over a minute, until all the loose material finally came to a stop in a huge mound in the middle of the courtyard. When the general peered up through the dissipating smoke, he could barely believe his eyes. The front side of the hill had been completely blown apart, revealing a gaping chasm hundreds of meters wide.

"Holy shit!" he exclaimed, slowly standing up to survey the carnage. "You weren't kidding about making a bigger explosion. But can this blow an entire *mountain* apart? The hills surrounding Thermopylae are quite a bit larger..."

"The size of the explosion will be commensurate with the quantity of explosive material used," Riley nodded. "If we space the holes closely enough apart, we should be able to make the entire ridge fall atop Xerxes' troops and bury them alive."

Leonidas peered up at the sky, noticing the sun beginning to disappear over the smoking hillside.

"We better bundle up our materials then," he said. "We've only got a couple more days to head off his army before it reaches the choke point. We'll need to head out at first light tomorrow morning."

Riley paused as she remembered the stakes concerning the battle that would change the course of western civilization.

"You should spend your last night with your beautiful wife," she said. "History has a way of surprising us. I don't know when or if you'll be able to return from this decisive clash."

The king paused as he noticed Dafni peering over the palace's balustrade at all the commotion below.

"Would you like to *join* the two of us?" he said. "Something tells me she'll want to enjoy our last encounter with *you* as much as she will with me."

"It will be my pleasure, general," Riley smiled, feeling a different kind of stirring in her loins. "Although I plan on doing everything in my power to ensure everybody's reunited after this momentous battle."

"I hope so," Leonidas said. "I don't know how you know all of these things before it happens, but I'm sure glad you're on *our* side."

Riley smiled, slipping her hand underneath his leather-trimmed skirt behind the privacy of his large shield still held in front of their two bodies.

"Actually, I was thinking we might *switch* sides this time," she said. "I've been thinking of a different way we can create a new kind of explosion tonight..."

10

W hen Riley and Leonidas returned to the palace, Dafni was waiting for them with a sumptuous spread laid out on their large dining table overlooking the valley. The courtyard was a mess, with piles of rubble strewn all about, but from their elevated position on the high ground over the city, the view from their location was still unobstructed and spectacular.

"That was quite an impressive demonstration," the queen said, sitting at the opposite end of the table from Leonidas. "Do you think it will be enough to stop Xerxes' army?"

"That remains to be seen," he said. "It depends on a lot of things, not the least of which is the ability of Riley's unique invention to work flawlessly when needed."

"I have confidence in her ability to perform," Dafni smiled. "She hasn't disappointed us yet."

"No," Leonidas nodded. "But I think you should prepare yourself, nonetheless. Everything's going to have to work perfectly, plus Xerxes mustn't get wind of what we've got planned. If his spies learn about our new weapons, it will prove difficult to lure him into our trap. We're still outnumbered twenty to one."

"Your soldiers are worth twenty of theirs," Dafni huffed. "They're fighting for their freedom, whereas most of Xerxes men are slaves, conscripted into the army. They won't have the same motivation to fight once the tables are turned against them."

"I hope you're right," the king said. "But let's stop all this talk of warmongering for a moment and enjoy a peaceful night of rest before setting off for battle in the morning."

The queen turned to peer at Riley, who was chewing her food pensively as she looked out over the valley.

"Will you be joining us again in our bedchamber this evening?" she said, caressing Riley's ankle under the table.

"I thought you might want to have some alone time on your last night together," Riley said. "I don't want to get in the way of your final tender moments..."

"Nonsense," the queen said. "You're practically part of the family now. Our lives are inextricably linked from this moment forward. Besides, I kind of like it when you get in the middle of our lovemaking. What do you say, Leo? Do you mind if Riley joins us for one more night?"

"I suppose not," Leonidas smiled. "Although I don't know how I'm going to satisfy both of you with only one *tool* at my disposal."

"Leave that up to us," the queen smiled. "I've been concocting my *own* little strategy while the two of you were playing with explosives in the courtyard."

∽

When the three lovers retired to the master bedroom after dinner, Dafni removed her clothing, then she laid face-up on the end of their bed with her legs spread apart.

"You fucked Riley well enough last time," she said to Leonidas. "Now it's *my* turn."

"What about our guest?" the king said as his big cock began to rise over his abdomen while he stared at his wife's shaved pussy. "How will she share in the fun?"

"I've got something *special* planned for her," Dafni said. "I've been dying to suck her pussy ever since I saw her naked in the bathtub. Come sit on my face while Leo fucks me from the front this time."

"Mmm," Riley purred, taking off her tunic and throwing it over the back of a nearby armchair. "I've been dreaming of planting my ass on your face from the moment I met you in the storeroom. Plus, I'll get to watch Leo...er, the king...close-up while he fucks your shaved pussy."

"I think we're way past all those formalities," Leonidas said, approaching the end of the bed and grasping Dafni's thighs as he pulled them further apart. "Leo is easier to say in the throes of moment, plus we may very well owe our very lives to you in the end. I think you can call us anything you want at this point."

"Okay, Leo," Riley smiled, climbing on top of Dafni and lowering her ass slowly onto her face. "Just do me one little favor. When you come, can you pull out so I can watch your beautiful cock spraying all over my tits?"

"I think that can be arranged," Leonidas grinned as his cock bobbed up and down between Dafni's legs while he watched Riley rubbing her pussy over his wife's wet face.

Dafni tilted her head to the side as she peered between Riley's glistening lips at her husband's dripping erection.

"Give me fair warning when you're getting close," she said. "I want to be the first one to come this time before you shoot off. Something tells me there's going to be a lot of fluid flying around before we finish our little tete-a-tete this evening."

"No worries," Leonidas groaned as he slipped his thick head into her opening and slowly slid his giant cock inside her hole.

"Fuck, yes," Dafni moaned as Riley began to roll her hips over her face. "This is so much better receiving stimulation on both ends. Your shaved pussy tastes like a ripe pomegranate."

"You're not the only one receiving stimulation from two sides," Riley panted as she watched Leonidas's glistening organ sliding in and out of the queen's shaved pussy. "Your husband is a magnificent specimen to watch."

"Just wait until you see him in *battle*," Dafni groaned, circling her legs over the back of his ass while Leonidas began to pound her harder. "He doesn't do anything halfway."

"So I can see," Riley huffed, watching the king sink his organ all the way into Dafni's bare pussy while the bed began to shake harder.

"I'm getting close," Dafni groaned as she squeezed Leonidas's hips. "Get ready for my signal–"

"I'm ready whenever you are," Leonidas huffed, staring at Riley's bouncing tits and her flushed face. "This is going to be big."

"Yes," Riley hissed, pressing her hips harder down onto the queen's face. "Suck my clit. I'm going to come so hard..."

"Oh fuck," the queen suddenly grunted, releasing her grip on the king's hips. "Now!"

Leonidas pulled his throbbing instrument out of his wife's slit and angled his hips upward as thick ropes of cum shot towards Riley's quivering torso, coating her breasts and nipples in a coat of creamy liquid. When Riley saw him coming over her tits, she tilted her head back and screamed at the top of her lungs, spraying her juices all over the queen's face while she sucked and lapped up her juices like a hungry puppy. It seemed to take almost a full minute for the three lovers to stop spurting their love juices over one another, and when they finally finished climaxing, they flopped down beside one another, holding each other tenderly.

"If that's the last time I make love to you," Leonidas said, cradling his wife's head. "I can die a happy man."

"Don't you dare," the queen said, reaching down to squeeze his balls firmly. "We're just getting started exploring the possibilities here."

"I can't imagine how many different ways the three of us can make love," the king said, reaching over to pull Riley closer to the two of them.

"Don't you worry about that, my king," Riley smiled. "Creating new weapons of war isn't the only thing I learned from my fancy schools on the other side of the world. Have you ever heard of the Kama Sutra? The Indians have invented *hundreds* of different ways for two or more people to have sex."

"Well, I guess we'll have a little extra motivation to win this looming clash with Xerxes, then," he smiled. "Because I'm tired of fighting battles. I'd rather make love than war."

11

———————

The following morning, Leonidas and Riley assembled his army for the long journey to the mountain pass of Thermopylae. They had to pack extra mules to carry the heavy pots of gunpowder and the smoldering cauldrons of naphtha, and by the time they were ready to set out, the train of assembled men and artillery was half a mile long.

"Please bring my husband back to me alive," Dafni whispered into Riley's ear as the general prepared to move out.

"Don't worry, my queen," Riley smiled. "When the other side sees the weapons of destruction we've prepared for them, they'll scurry back where they came from soon enough."

Dafni nodded, then she turned around to face Leonidas with tears in her eyes.

"And you, you big brute," she said, choking up. "Make sure you bring that beautiful cock of yours back to me undamaged. I don't know what I'd do with myself if I didn't have you to keep my bed warm at night."

"I'm sure you'd find some other willing partners to keep

yourself amused before too long," the king chuckled. "But don't worry, my cock and I have plenty of plans for keeping you entertained after I return."

"Good luck, my love," Dafni said, giving Leonidas a long kiss on his lips. "You too, my sexy new friend," she said, giving Riley a peck on the side of her cheek.

"We'll be back long before your bed becomes cold," Riley nodded.

Leonidas hopped on his horse and raised his arm, signaling for his troops to begin moving forward. As he and Riley set out at the head of the column side-by-side, Dafni blew them both a silent kiss.

After a few miles of pensive riding, the king turned to Riley with a worried expression on his face.

"What is it, Leo?" Riley said, beginning to feel comfortable addressing the king as a friend and equal.

"We never got around to equipping our *navy* to repel Xerxes' ships," he said. "They're almost as outnumbered as we are. If they break through Themistocles' defenses, there'll be nothing to stop them from overrunning Athens."

"Don't worry," Riley nodded. "I've already taken care of it. I've instructed your aide to deliver the recipe for Greek Fire to your commander of the fleet."

"I'm not sure those *grenades* will be sufficient to repel his ships. The oarsmen will be too busy maneuvering the vessels and the rest of his men will need to be prepared to repel the boarding party."

"I've given Milos instructions for preparing a *different* kind of delivery mechanism," Riley said.

"What kind?" Leonidas said, pinching his eyebrows

together. "Some kind of *catapult*? They'll hardly have enough time to reload before Xerxes brings his ships broadside..."

"I've instructed Milo how to build a *siphon* that will store large quantities of the liquid that can be sprayed on the enemy ships from a distance. The opposing sailors shouldn't be able to get close enough to board your vessels."

"How exactly are you going to do that?" Leonidas said, peering ahead at the tall mountains overlooking the pass of Thermopylae in the distance. "Will they have enough time to build these devices?"

"They can build them out of two pieces of bamboo," Riley nodded. "One piece to store the volatile liquid and the other, slightly narrower one to slide in and out of the thicker tube. It should work like a large syringe, squirting the flammable fluid out of its nozzle in metered doses. Once the fluid in the syringe is emptied, it will be easy to reload by dipping the tip into the vats of naphtha and pulling the plunger in the opposite direction."

"That's ingenious," the king nodded, peering at the upcoming valley with renewed confidence. "Where did you ever learn all this specialized knowledge?"

"At a special school for engineers in America," Riley smiled. "But I've always been a bit of a nerd, studying chemistry and mechanics long before I enrolled at MIT."

"This place called *America* sounds like a forbidding empire," Leonidas said. "They must have grown quite successful using all this modern technology."

"They've become the dominant power of the day," Riley nodded. "But none of it would have been possible without the groundwork laid by the ancient civilization of Greece. Thanks to your democratic form of government and your arresting of the forces of Islam, the West was allowed to prosper and advance their technology in the first place."

"Well, it's technically the government of *Athens* that developed the institutions of democracy," Leonidas frowned. "Sparta is still technically a monarchy, with me as the sole governing leader."

"That may be true," Riley said. "But I've seen how you rule with a gentle hand. Your men are willing to put their very lives at stake to protect everything you've built and let you lead them into battle."

"I guess they're about to find out exactly how capable their leader is," he said, watching the mountains in the distance looming ever closer. "If we don't prevail over Xerxes' forces, everything we've built will be quickly lost."

"Leave that to me," Riley said. "But if we defeat him at Thermopylae, you might want to consider adopting the Athenian model. It will relieve the pressure of managing your kingdom all alone, and you'll be able to live a much quieter life. You said yourself that you'd rather make love than war."

"If you can help both me and the Greek navy defeat Xerxes' forces, I'll be only too happy to retire," Leonidas nodded. "With these new weapons of war, nobody will dare attacking us again."

"That's the plan, general," Riley sighed atop her horse next to the general. "That's the plan."

12

When Leonidas and his army reached the pass, he instructed half of his men to position themselves at the north-facing entrance to the valley, then he divided the rest of his troops toward the opposing sides of the mountains framing the pass to cut off a potential outflanking by the enemy. While his soldiers began to dig pits halfway up the mountain on both sides of the pass, Leonidas and a few of his men walked up one of the narrow trails with Riley to view the surrounding countryside from a higher elevation.

When they got near the top of the ridge, the king paused and turned his body toward the north, placing his palm over his forehead as he peered into the distance. But what he saw on the horizon made his stomach turn over in sickness. Xerxes' army was marching toward his position like a giant swarm of ants, seemingly a million-strong. The column of soldiers and horses was so huge, it seemed to fill his entire field of vision, with no end to the marching convoy creating a huge cloud of dust in their wake.

"It's even worse than I thought," he said, turning toward

Riley with a worried expression. "His army is so large, it's as if the entire *landscape* is moving. I can't see how we can possibly stop such an imposing force."

"If everything goes according to plan, you won't have to," Riley said, peering out at the looming horde with wide eyes. "We're going to use the advantage of the topography of the pass to squeeze his army into the valley, then use my explosives to cut them off on two sides. The exploding grenades should do the rest of the work to finish them off."

"It's the *if* part of that that worries me," the general said. "If this doesn't work exactly as you demonstrated, we'll be trapped alongside them, missing the chance to use our phalanx formation to keep them at bay."

"It will be better to keep them below you from higher ground," Riley nodded, remembering the climactic moment in the famous movie The Three Hundred, where Leonidas's last stand of remaining troops succumbed to the overwhelming onslaught of Xerxes' invading forces. "Once you begin raining Greek Fire down upon them, they'll be unable to get out of the closed-off area and will perish in the flames."

"It sounds almost too perfect to believe," Leonidas said, motioning for his officers to begin preparing the men. "Why don't we inspect the placement of the explosives to make sure everything is in position? You should be able to judge better than anyone how successful our plan is likely to be."

"Yes..." Riley nodded, afraid to admit to the general just how unsure she felt about the prospects of her explosives toppling an entire mountain.

$\sim$

After Riley and Leonidas finished inspecting the location of the explosives and the positioning of his men, they returned to the base of the valley to join the main contingent of his forces waiting at the entrance to the pass, to prepare them for the upcoming confrontation.

"We're about to face the greatest test in the history of our great army," he announced to his troops. "When you see the advancing enemy, it will seem that we are facing impossible odds. But I prevail upon you to keep your wits and remember your training. We have the advantage of superior terrain and weapons the enemy has never seen before."

Leonidas passed while he surveyed the look of determination on his hardened soldiers. They'd participated in many battles previously, and most of the time they'd come away bloodied but victorious. But they all knew this was going to be a confrontation like nothing they'd ever faced before.

"When they advance to our position," he continued. "It will be tempting to withdraw. But we need to engage them with all of our combined might in order to lure them into our trap. Once they see the imbalance in our forces, they will try to quickly overrun us. But in the narrow confines of the pass, they will be unable to surround us. Use the protective shield of your phalanx formation to keep them at bay while you slowly retreat into the pocket between the mountains..."

Leonidas' men were so enthralled listening to his inspiring speech that you could barely hear a pin drop among the thousands of soldiers who were hinging on his every word. While Riley peered out at the mass of muscled soldiers wearing their shiny brass armor and wraparound helmets, her pussy throbbed watching the general leading his men with so much confidence. In spite of the overwhelming odds, he hadn't hesitated to volunteer leading his army into a battle where it seemed certain everybody would perish. She'd tilted the odds slightly in his favor, but the mere magnitude of the opposing army seemed utterly unsurmountable. One way or the other, this would be their last stand, and the fate of western civilization rested on their ability to repel the invading horde and save the rest of Europe from enslavement at the hands of the Persian empire.

"When you hear the explosions from the opposite sides of the valley," Leonidas instructed his men. "This will be your cue to retreat to higher ground. Join your countrymen from their hidden positions on the embankment and use the grenades to fling fire down upon the trapped soldiers. When they see they have no escape and that our Greek Fire clings to them like sticky molasses, they will quickly give up the fight and run for their lives. Our proud army will prevail once again, and this battle will go down in the annals of history as one of the greatest victories of our time. When we return to our villages, we can lay down our arms once and for all, knowing that we can live as free men without the fear of encroaching armies taking over our country. We will *fight* like Spartans and *die* like Spartans!"

"Hoo-ha!" his regiment yelled in unison, raising their swords over their head and pumping their arms in excitement.

Leonidas paused as he surveyed his confident troops, allowing a small smile to form on his lips. When he peered over at Riley for a brief moment, it took all of her power not to jump on top of him and pull his big phallus out from under his leather skirt and fuck him where he stood.

∼

L ater that night, as a peaceful pall fell over the valley, Leonidas and Riley retreated into his tent while the rest of his men slept quietly on their blankets with their shields propped up as improvised pillows.

"That was quite a speech you made earlier today," Riley said, sliding her hand over the general's muscular shoulder.

"I hope it was enough to steel their nerve when the time comes," Leonidas said. "When they come face-to-face with the overwhelming size of Xerxes' army, their confidence will quickly evaporate."

"But you've trained them well," Riley nodded. "And the size of his troops won't matter once they're squeezed into the narrow pass. It will be man against man, and your men are better equipped and better trained. They just need to hold them off long enough for our new weapons to do their job."

"Yes," Leonidas said. "I never properly thanked you for everything you've done to help us. Without your assistance, we would have never stood a chance against Xerxes' army."

"Don't thank me yet," Riley said. "There's a lot of moving parts to our battle plan. There's still a lot that can go wrong..."

"True," the general said. "But we've done everything we can to prepare. Now it's time to get a good night's rest before we face the enemy in the morning light."

"Are you sure you want to rest right away?" Riley grinned, pulling off her tunic and rubbing her naked body up against the general's shiny breastplate and the leather flaps of his skirt. "Perhaps we can get your testosterone stirring in preparation for the battle..."

"Testosterone–?" Leonidas said, caressing the tips of her nipples.

"Never mind," Riley smiled, grabbing hold of his rising organ pressing out from under his flared battle skirt. "It's just another name for one of our newfangled chemicals. Albeit one that makes both of our libidos work overtime, increasing our desire for things other than war..."

13

———————

Early the following morning, one of the general's aides tapped on the entrance to his tent, announcing that Xerxes' army had massed near the front of the pass. Leonidas and Riley got up and went to their lookout, where they appraised the standoff between the two forces. The Persian army stretched out for miles into the distance, tapering into a bottleneck near the gate like grains of sand in an overturned hourglass.

"The size of their army doesn't seem to end," Leonidas said to Riley, peering out at the long column of soldiers stretching out behind them.

"But they still need to squeeze through this pass to reach Athens and Sparta," Riley nodded. "Their superiority in numbers won't make much difference as long as you can keep them contained."

The king paused as he glanced down the valley at his camouflaged soldiers waiting on the hillsides with their improvised grenades.

"Are you sure your explosives are going to work?" he said with a worried expression.

"They should work well enough to loosen the rocks and hail debris down upon the opposing army," Riley said. "At the very least, it will create enough chaos in their ranks to pause their advance and allow your men time to deploy the grenades."

Moments later, another one of the general's aides approached him, handing him a note scratched on parchment.

"What is it?" Riley said, recognizing the Greek symbols on the paper.

"It's a message from Xerxes," he said, scanning the text. "He's asking for us to surrender. If we reject his ultimatum, he says he'll demolish our forces and kill all the women and children of Sparta."

"You're not seriously considering his proposal?" Riley said, watching the king's face as he surveyed the size of the opposing forces.

"Of course not," Leonidas said, scrunching up the letter and flinging it onto the ground.

"What are you going to do?" Riley said.

"Exactly what we planned," the general said. "But first, I'm going to send him a little message of my own."

He whispered something into the ear of one of his lieutenants, and the soldier scurried down the hill toward the vanguard of his battalion, which had positioned themselves into a V-shape formation, with their huge shields placed side-by-side to create an impenetrable barrier.

"Stay here with a few of my aides," he said, turning toward Riley. "I'll give the signal when it's time to set off the explosives."

"Where are you going?" Riley said, flaring her eyes as Leonidas turned away to join the rest of his men on the lower ground.

"I'm the leader of the Spartan army," he said. "What kind of general would I be if I kept myself out of the fray and left all the fighting to my soldiers?"

"But, their army...?" Riley said, trying to convince the king to stay out of harm's way while he directed the action from higher up the hillside. "You won't be able to stop them—"

"We don't need to stop them," Leonidas said. "We just need to make them think we intend to fight them to the end. Your weapons will turn the tables once we've lured them far enough into our trap."

"Be careful," Riley said, reaching out her hand to touch his arm. The queen will never forgive me if I don't return you alive."

"Don't worry about me," he smiled. "This isn't the first time we've faced insurmountable odds. My men are well trained and we've got a solid plan in place. I'll see you when the dust settles."

Riley watched Leonidas descend the mountain and join his men at the tip of the phalanx, then he raised his hand and motioned toward his archers waiting in the rearguard position. Seconds later, a hail of arrows arched high over the front of his formation, raining down on the lightly dressed Persian soldiers lined up at the front of Xerxes' army. There were a few screams, and some of the opposing soldiers fell onto the ground mortally wounded, then there was a brief pause before Xerxes' much larger group of archers returned fire.

The sky suddenly turned black from the mass of arrows heading toward Leonidas's position, and he and the rest of his men crouched down, holding their shields over their heads while the spiked sticks thudded into their thick wooden coverings. Seconds later, there was a roar from

Xerxes' army as they surged forward, trying to overrun the much smaller group of Greek warriors huddled together in their V-formation. But the Persians were no match for the more heavily armed Greek warriors, as Leonidas's men speared them with their long spikes from the protection of their impenetrable shell.

After a few minutes, the sheer weight of the Persian army pressing forward from behind began to push Leonidas's front line slowly backwards, creeping into the pass one meter at a time while the general tried to maintain the integrity of his formation, leading the bulk of Xerxes' army into the narrow valley until it was teeming with moving heads from one end to the other. When Leonidas's men reached the opposite end of the valley, he suddenly stood up, waving his sword over his head while his soldiers broke apart and began scurrying up the hillsides.

At first, Xerxes didn't know what to make of their cowardly attempt to flee, then after a few moments, he ordered his men to take chase. But seconds later, a series of large explosions rocked the two ends of the valley, and the earth began to rumble and fall apart as huge landslides rained down upon his men, trapping the rest of his forces in the narrow enclosure of the canyon. The Persian soldiers paused their chase for a few moments, worried that the rest of the mountain might fall down upon them, then the Greek soldiers waiting in the bushes stood up, igniting their hand-held grenades and hurling them down upon the helpless infantry. The fragile clay pots exploded on contact and the sticky pine resin mixed into the formula stuck to their bodies, making it impossible to extinguish the burning flames on their skin. The Persian soldiers screamed in pain, rolling down the hillsides like a bunch of bowling balls, taking down scores of their countrymen and setting the rest of the trapped forces aflame.

As Riley watched the carnage unfold and listened to the screams of pain from the terrorized Persian soldiers, she had to look away, sickened at the thought of what she'd unleashed on the huge army of unsuspecting fighters. While Leonidas's men continued to rain flaming pots onto the unprepared Persians, she leaned over and vomited onto the ground beside her. A few moments later, the general appeared by her side, holding her shoulders as she heaved her body in violent lurches.

"Are you alright?" he said with a worried expression. "Have you been injured?"

"Only my *pride*," Riley said, standing up and surveying the swarm of opposing soldiers twisting in pain on the ground, unable to find shelter from the hail of exploding canisters raining down all around them. "It sickens me to see all this pain and suffering."

"It's unfortunate," Leonidas said, watching his men throwing down the last volley of fiery grenades. "But it was us or them. They would have tortured us just as severely if we'd lost the battle. War is messy, and pain and misery is a necessary consequence of two armies battling to the death."

"But most of those soldiers are just slaves, fighting because they've been *forced* to," Riley said. "They never signed up for any of this like your volunteer army. It's sad to see them perish this way."

"Our women and children would have been slaves too," the general nodded. "We were simply defending ourselves and our families from a tyrant who would stop at nothing to expand his empire. Like you said yourself, without the resolve of our Greek soldiers, the entire face of western civilization would have forever been changed."

"I suppose you're right," Riley said, clasping Leonidas's hand while he squeezed it reassuringly. "I just hope Themistocles was equally successful fending off Xerxes' navy in the straits of Artemisium."

14

After the Greek soldiers vanquished Xerxes' army, they headed back toward Sparta, laughing and joking amongst themselves about how much of a pushover the vaunted Persian army had been. But Riley knew better, trotting slowly next to Leonidas atop her horse while she pondered how easily it could have gone the other way.

"You don't seem as happy as the rest of my men about the outcome of the battle," the king said, noticing Riley's contemplative mood.

"It's not that," Riley said. "I just remember how history recalled this scene. I don't want your soldiers to get too complacent. The Ottomans will return to contest your territory many times again. You may have won this battle, but the war will continue for many centuries to come."

"But didn't we just *rewrite* history?" Leonidas said, squinting at Riley. "At least this particular chapter? Haven't your weapons turned the tide in our favor?"

Suddenly, a soldier galloped up to the side of the general's horse, handing him a scroll with a wax seal. Leonidas paused as he unfolded the scroll to read the contents. After a few seconds, a smile began to form on his lips and he peered over at Riley, nodding happily.

"What is it?" she said.

"It's a note from Themistocles," the king said. "He was able to turn away most of Xerxes' ships with the help of your ingenious invention. Our country appears to be safe from the invasion of the pagans, at least for now."

Riley nodded as she remembered how the Greeks had used the invention of Greek Fire for hundreds of years to successfully fend off repeated incursions of the eastern armies.

"Please advise him to keep the formula carefully hidden and protected," she said. "That concoction is the only thing keeping the enemy from overrunning your lands with complete impunity."

"I will," Leonidas said. "Thanks to you, our citizens can sleep safely tonight, knowing they'll be able to resist anyone who tries to attack them again."

"Think nothing of it," Riley smiled. "I'm just glad I was in the right place at the right time."

When Leonidas's troops returned to Sparta, the townspeople swarmed into the square, surrounded them like conquering heroes and jumping up and down with unrestrained happiness while they kissed their sons and husbands with tears streaming down their faces. The queen descended the steps from the palace wearing Riley's kimono, and when the king hopped off his horse, she wrapped her arms around his neck, giving him a long, lingering kiss.

"I hope you don't mind my wearing your robe these past few days," Dafni smiled toward Riley, who was watching the amorous couple with a flush in her face. "It helped me remember you while you were away. Plus, this fabric feels absolutely heavenly against my skin."

"I'm glad you like it," Riley said. "I'll be happy to leave it for you when it's time for me to move on. I expect I won't be needing it for the remainder of my travels."

"I hope you won't be leaving us *too* soon," the queen frowned. "Our staff is preparing an enormous feast to celebrate your victory at Thermopylae."

"I'd like to make Riley our guest of honor," Leonidas nodded. "Without her help, none of us would have been able to make it back alive."

"It's decided then," the queen said. "If you can have your men clear out the courtyard, I'll get started with the preparations right away."

Leonidas reached out and grabbed Dafni's arm, winking at her softly.

"Do you think it can wait another hour or so?" he said. "I've worked up quite an appetite for a different kind of celebration after our long journey home."

"You're reading my mind," Dafni smiled, noticing the bulge in his battle skirt while she peered over in Riley's direction. "Do you want to join us?"

"I think you two deserve to be alone this time," Riley smiled, noticing the maids preparing a large spread on the dining table overlooking the valley. "If you don't mind, I'll quench my appetite with a little wine and some fresh figs for the time being."

"Of course," the king said, smiling at his wife. "Help yourself to anything you want. If it wasn't for you, *none* of us would be enjoying any of the fruits of our labors."

"Will you join us *tonight*, then?" Dafni said, opening the flap of her kimono partway to reveal her erect nipples. "I've been dreaming of an entirely new way for the three of us to amuse ourselves later this evening."

"You're twisting my arm," Riley smiled, feeling her pussy twitching between her legs.

"That's not the *only* thing we'll be twisting tonight," the queen said, grabbing Leonidas's hand and dragging him up the stairs in the direction of their master bedroom.

⁓

Over the next couple of hours, Leonidas's soldiers cleared the last of the rubble from the courtyard, then they built an enormous bonfire in the middle of the square, with heaping plates of roast pig, braised lamb and Mediterranean salad laid out in concentric circles for all the townspeople to enjoy. When the king and queen emerged from the palace, he paused near the top of the steps to address his subjects.

"To my brave soldiers and countrymen," he said, lifting a large chalice of wine. "Without your courage and determination, none of this would be possible."

A huge cheer rose from the crowd assembled in the square, then Leonidas raised his hand to stifle their cries.

"But a special thanks goes to one young lady who appeared in our midst like an angel from the heavens," he said, pointing toward Riley, who had joined the crowd in the courtyard. "I don't know how she found us or where she learned her mystical skills, but without her help, this battle and the one fought by our allies near Athens would have surely been lost. Let us raise a glass to our honorary guest, *Riley from America!*"

"The crowd lifted their glasses and pumped their arms vigorously over their heads, chanting her name while the girl blushed.

"Ri-lee, Ri-lee, Ri-lee!" they shouted in unison.

After another minute or so, the king raised his hand once again to interrupt their delirious celebration.

"I have one other announcement to make," he said, lowering his voice solemnly. "From this point forward, I will no longer your king. From now on, your leader will be chosen by a plebiscite of the people, overseen by a group of legislators that will approve and enact those laws deemed of benefit for the people. You are now *truly* free men and women, charting your own destiny and setting an example for the rest of the world!"

"Woo-hoo!!" everybody cheered as they began to dance happily in circles around the fire while Dafni and Leonidas quietly looked on.

"Are you *sure* you want to do this?" she said, peering at her husband. "You're likely to lose a few perks of your office, like having the palace all to yourself–"

"It was too big for the two of us anyhow," he smiled, grabbing hold of her hand. "Let's join the rest of our people and enjoy the celebration. From now on, we're just ordinary citizens."

When they stepped down into the courtyard, they held out their arms and mingled with the rest of the townspeople, dancing around the fire with joyous expressions. When they saw Riley weaving through the crowd, Dafni snared her arm and pulled her next to the ex-king and queen.

"Are you ready for a *different* kind of celebration?" she grinned, squeezing Riley's ass. "You must be eager for a soft bed and some warm companionship after riding atop a bumpy horse for most of the day."

"Absolutely," Riley smiled, noticing Leonidas's swelling organ darting the bottom of his tunic, reaching almost down to the top of his knees. "But where will we *sleep* tonight, now that the king has abdicated the throne? I don't imagine they're going to let him continue using the palace now that he's no longer the king..."

"They haven't elected a new leader *yet*," Dafni said, grabbing hold of both their hands and dragging them back in the direction of the palace. "I don't think they'll mind us using it for one more night, especially when they see their new goddess of war keeping watch over them."

15

———

When Dafni, Leonidas, and Riley stumbled into the king's bedroom, they tore off their clothes and tumbled into the bed, laughing and rolling their bodies together in unbridled glee. At first, they just groped and kissed each other wantonly, then Dafni rolled Leonidas over onto his back with his big erection flapping excitedly over his belly.

"Mmm," he panted, watching the two women caressing his throbbing organ. "Are you going to take *turns* fucking me this time?"

"Don't get too ahead of yourself, big boy," Dafni chuckled. "*Riley's* our guest of honor tonight, remember?"

"Right," Leonidas nodded. "What can I do to give her the proper attention she deserves?"

"Well, to start with," Dafni smiled. "Why don't you let *her* be on top this time? I was thinking she could sit on your cock facing away, while I lick her pussy and your balls at the same time. That is, if she's amenable to a little more male attention this evening..."

"I don't mind if I do," Riley grinned, squatting over Leonidas's thick instrument and slowly lowering herself onto his pulsating organ. "That's one way we haven't tried yet..."

"Oh?" Dafni said, kneeling between their legs. "Have you two been *practicing* while I've been away?"

"Maybe once or twice," Riley grunted as she rocked her hips over Leonidas's tightening balls. "I couldn't let him go into battle without one last reminder of what he had to fight for."

"Indeed," Dafni nodded, lowering her face to tickle Riley's clit while her husband pounded her pussy. "I don't mind a bit. After all, we're one big happy family now."

"Oh God," Riley panted, tilting her torso a few degrees backwards to give Dafni freer access to her glistening vulva.

While Leonidas rubbed his balls against her chin, Dafni didn't hesitate to bury her face in Riley's crotch.

"I'm going to miss this beautiful pussy after you're gone," she said. "Are you *sure* you have to leave us so soon?"

"Let's not worry about that right now," Riley groaned, lowering her back onto Leonidas's chest while he reached around and squeezed her tits. "Let's just enjoy the moment. The future can wait."

"Thanks to you, it'll be a lot more peaceful," Dafni said, beginning to crawl atop Riley and Leonidas on all fours.

She lowered her body onto Riley's writhing body, then she slipped her tongue into her mouth as she began to grind her bare pussy against their rocking hips.

"Ungghh," Riley moaned when she felt Dafni and Leonidas fucking her from opposite sides. "I'm going to miss this–"

"And I'm going to miss your smooth kolpos," Dafni

panted as she ground their clits together while Leonidas peered up at her flushed face.

"Maybe you can have Leo shave you next time," Riley huffed, feeling a powerful orgasm slowly building up inside her belly. "It can be a very erotic activity between two partners."

"I like that idea," Dafni groaned, pressing her pussy harder against their rocking hips. "Maybe I'll do *him,* too. I'd love to see his magnificent tool in all its natural glory."

"Oh my God," Riley hissed, feeling herself falling over the precipice. "That's too hot to imagine. Can I do it *with* you?"

"Of course," Dafni smiled while she squeezed the sides of Riley's ass tighter. "But right now, there's something *else* I need to finish first. I'm going to come so hard over your balls and pussy..."

"Fuck, yes," Riley squealed, stiffening her legs and arching her back upward. *"Nnngahhh!"*

When Riley began squirting her juices over Leonidas's balls and Dafni's pussy, the three lovers grasped each other tightly, holding one to one another as they convulsed their bodies together and kissed each other's faces, groaning in one another's ears. When they finally stopped shaking a few minutes later and lay still in each other's arms, they listened to the sound of the townspeople partying in the lower court-yard while they whooped and hollered around the fire.

My work is done here, Riley smiled to herself as she reveled in the feeling of the retired king and queen lying peacefully in each other's arms without a care in the world.

$\sim$

After they fell asleep later that night, Riley crept out of their bedroom and made her way to her old guest quarters. She brought a chair to the corner of the armoire and stepped up onto it to retrieve her magic smartphone hidden on top of the cabinet. Then she sat down in front of her make-up table to compose a short note to her new friends.

Dear Leo and Dafni,

Thank you for welcoming me into your beautiful village and allowing me to assist in the campaign to turn away your adversaries. Nothing makes me happier to know that you and the rest of your countrymen will be safe for centuries to come with the aid of the new technology that your people were actually the first to invent.

I will miss both of you terribly, but I know that you will be happy in your roles as equal citizens within the new democratic framework you've established. But rest assured, my king, your legacy as the bravest of Greek soldiers will survive for centuries to come.

Antio, fíloi mou,

Riley

P.S.: I've left my kimono for Dafni to wear and remember me by, as I won't be needing it the next place I visit. May your skin tingle whenever you wear it next to your bare skin...

Riley placed some rose petals around the finished letter, then she pulled on her Greek tunic and sandals, sitting on the edge of the bed while she tapped the screen of her smartphone. After a few seconds, the familiar swirl of a twisting funnel appeared on the surface, then the device began to shake violently as the 3-D apparition rose above the screen. She placed her fingers at the top of the vortex, then she began to feel her body pulled into the cyclone while she glanced out the window at the dancing crowd below.

Within seconds, she felt herself tumbling through the time-travel portal again, wondering where she'd land next. After a few minutes, the flashing lights changed into a searing overhead sun as she felt her body drop down into a thronging market filled with swarthy men wearing colorful turbans and women covered in full-body burkas.

Suddenly, a fresh peach fell onto the ground in front of her, rolling toward her upturned body. She peered up and saw two women staring down at her like she was an alien from another planet. Even though they were both covered from head to toe in their full-body suits, Riley could see through their narrow eye slits that one of them was older and the other was quite young.

She stood up and handed the peach to the younger girl, and the girl nodded her head as she smiled back at her with her dazzling green eyes.

"Shukran," she said, lifting out her delicate hand to receive the fruit from Riley.

"Min dawaei sururi," Riley said in flawless Arabic, telling the girl it was her pleasure.

Then the older woman grabbed the girl's arm and turned away, dragging her down the busy thoroughfare while roadside vendors scurried about, hawking their wares.

What have I gotten myself into now? Riley thought to herself as the Arab men scowled at her uncovered head and bare legs, shaking their heads disapprovingly.

Ready for more steamy time travel adventures? Read the next exciting volume in Riley's Time Travel Adventures, *Arabian Nights. Buy direct and save at victoriarusherotica. Or download from your favorite online bookstore here: retailer links.*

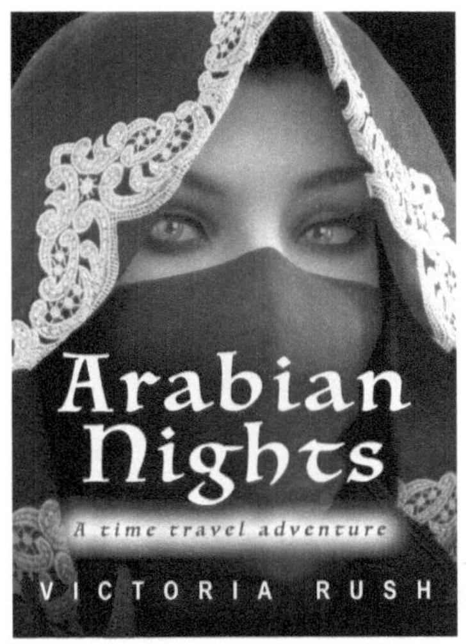

Forbidden love is often the most intense love...

ALSO BY VICTORIA RUSH

Adult Fairytales:

The Enchanted Forest: An Erotic Fairytale

The Land of Giants: An Erotic Fairytale

The Dragon's Lair: An Erotic Fairytale

Witch's Brew: An Erotic Fairytale

The Mage's Spell: An Erotic Fairytale

The Mermaid Lagoon: An Erotic Fairytale

The Coven: An Erotic Fairytale

Rapunzel: An Erotic Fairytale

The Seven Dwarfs: An Erotic Fairytale

The Land of Mutants: An Erotic Fairytale

The Erotic Temple: A Sexy Fairytale (Coming Soon)

Erotica Themed Bundles:

Voyeur: Lesbian Erotica Bundle

Public Affairs: A Lesbian Anthology

Futa Fantasies: The Ladyboy Collection

Threesomes: The Lesbian Collection

Threesomes - Volume 2: The Lesbian Collection

First Time: A Lesbian Anthology

Hedonism: An Erotic Anthology

Switch Hitters: Bisexual Erotica

Taboo Erotica: The Lesbian Series

BDSM: The Lesbian Collection

Party Games: The Erotic Collection

Party Games 2: The Erotic Collection

All Girl 1: Lesbian Erotica Bundle

All Girl 2: Lesbian Erotica Bundle

All Girl 3: Lesbian Erotica Bundle

All Girl 4: Lesbian Erotica Bundle

Erotic Fairytale Bundles:

Clover's Fantasy Adventures: Books 1 - 5

Clover's Fantasy Adventures: Books 6 - 10

Erotic Fantasy:

Pirate's Bounty: A Time Travel Adventure

Wild West: A Time Travel Adventure

Private Riley: A Time Travel Adventure

Cleopatra's Secret: A Time Travel Adventure

Bounty Hunter 2125: A Time Travel Adventure

Ninja Assassin: A Time Travel Adventure

The 300: A Time Travel Adventure

Arabian Nights: An Erotic Fairytale (coming soon...)

Steamy Time Travel Bundles:

Riley's Time Travel Adventures: Books 1 - 5

Lesbian Erotica:

The Dinner Party: Lesbian Voyeur Erotica

The Darkroom: Bisexual Voyeur Erotica

Naked Yoga: Lesbian Transgender Erotica

Nude Cruise: Bisexual Voyeur Erotica

Rush Hour: Taboo Public Sex

The Girl Next Door: First Time Lesbian Erotic Romance

Girls' Camp: Lesbian Group Sex

Wet Dream: Ladyboy Fantasy Erotica

The Convent: Taboo Sex with a Nun

Sex Robot: A Dream Sex Machine

The Personal Trainer: Getting Pumped at the Gym

The Dominatrix: BDSM Lesbian Domination

Webcam Chat: Lesbian Online Sex

Paint Me: A Kinky Bodypainting Workshop

The Toy Party: Girls Sharing Sex Toys

The Costume Party: Strapping One On

Swedish Sauna: Lesbian Group Sex

The Therapist: Taboo Lesbian Erotica

Elevator Shaft: Bisexual Threesomes Erotica

Ladyboy: Lesbian Transgender Erotica

Peep Show: Lesbian Voyeur Erotica

The Dare: Public Sex Erotica

Maid Service: Lesbian Threesomes Erotica

The Hitchhiker: First Time Lesbian Erotica

The Housesitter: Spycam Lesbian Erotica

The Spa: Lesbian Group Orgy

Parlor Games: Blindfold Sex Party

The Exchange Student: First Time Lesbian Erotica

The Hostel: Bisexual Group Erotica

The Harem: Lesbian Erotic Romance

The Orient Express: Lesbian Voyeur Erotica

The First Lady: A Forbidden Lesbian Erotic Romance

The Slave: Lesbian BDSM Erotica

The Masseuse: Lesbian Sensuous Erotica

Too Close for Comfort: Lesbian Forbidden Erotica

Naked Twister: A Wild Party Game

Lexi: The Sex App (Lesbian Fantasy Erotica)

Call Girl: Lesbian Bisexual Threesomes Erotica

Circle Jill: Lesbian Masturbation Workshop

The Viewing Room: Masturbation Voyeur Erotica

Spin the Bottle: A Kinky Party Game

The Hair Salon: Lesbian Voyeur Erotica

Tribadism 1: Girls Only Sex Workshop

Tribadism 2: The Art of Scissoring

Tribadism 3: Threeway Hookups

The Kiss: A Game of Oral Sex

Pledge Week: Sorority Sisters

Carny Games 1: A Wild Sex Party

Carny Games 2: A Kinky Sex Party

Carny Games 3: An Erotic Sex Party

Dreamscape: An Artificial Reality Game

Glory Hole: Guess Who's On the Other Side

Joy Ride: A Late Night Erotic Bus Trip

The Blind Girl: An Erotic Romance(Coming Soon)

Lesbian Erotica Bundles:

Jade's Erotic Adventures: Books 1 - 5

Jade's Erotic Adventures: Books 6 - 10

Jade's Erotic Adventures: Books 11 - 15

Jade's Erotic Adventures: Books 16 - 20

Jade's Erotic Adventures: Books 21 - 25

Jade's Erotic Adventures: Books 26 - 30

Jade's Erotic Adventures: Books 31 - 35

Jade's Erotic Adventures: Books 36 - 40

Jade's Erotic Adventures: Books 41 - 45

Jade's Erotic Adventures: Books 46 - 50

Fifty Shades of Jade: Superbundle

Standalone Stories:

The Polynesian Girl: A Lesbian EroticRomance

FOLLOW VICTORIA RUSH:

Want to keep informed of my latest erotic book releases? Sign up for my newsletter and receive a FREE bonus book:

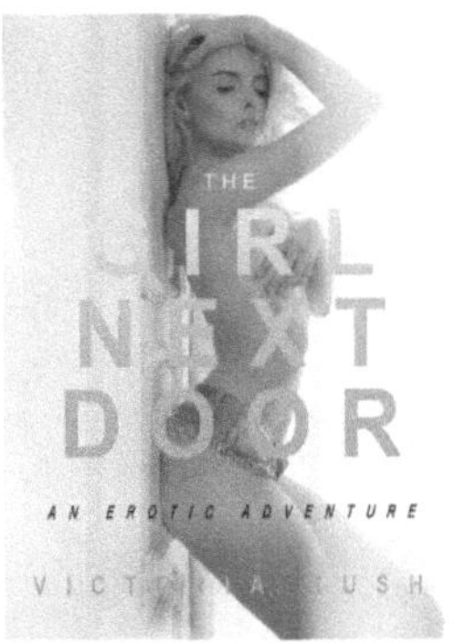

Spying on the neighbors just got a lot more interesting...